To all the big and little people
who inspire peace on earth

AMDG

At day's end, when the sun has done its job and darkness has nearly covered the land, a great and gentle light rises in the night to take its place.

Some children call it
Luna. Others name it *Lune*.
But you know it as the *Moon*!

The moon is nature's friend.

Our moon helps push the oceans' tides;

guides loggerhead turtles as they lay their eggs;

**assists salmon as they make
their way to the sea;**

leads the large underwing moth as it travels across the English countryside;

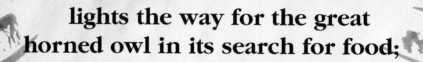

**lights the way for the great
horned owl in its search for food;**

**and smiles kindly on us with
its soft night light.**

**But there is something even more
wonderful about the moon's light.**

It can even help to make a miracle.

You see, if you cup your hands on a moonlit night, where the moon's light enters your window, you can really and truly hold a piece of moonbeam right where you are.

But best of all, if in all the
world each boy and girl would
capture a moonbeam, they would
become linked together by
holding onto the very same light.

And they would then understand that moonbeams are one of God's many miracles helping us see that we are all brothers and sisters in one human family.